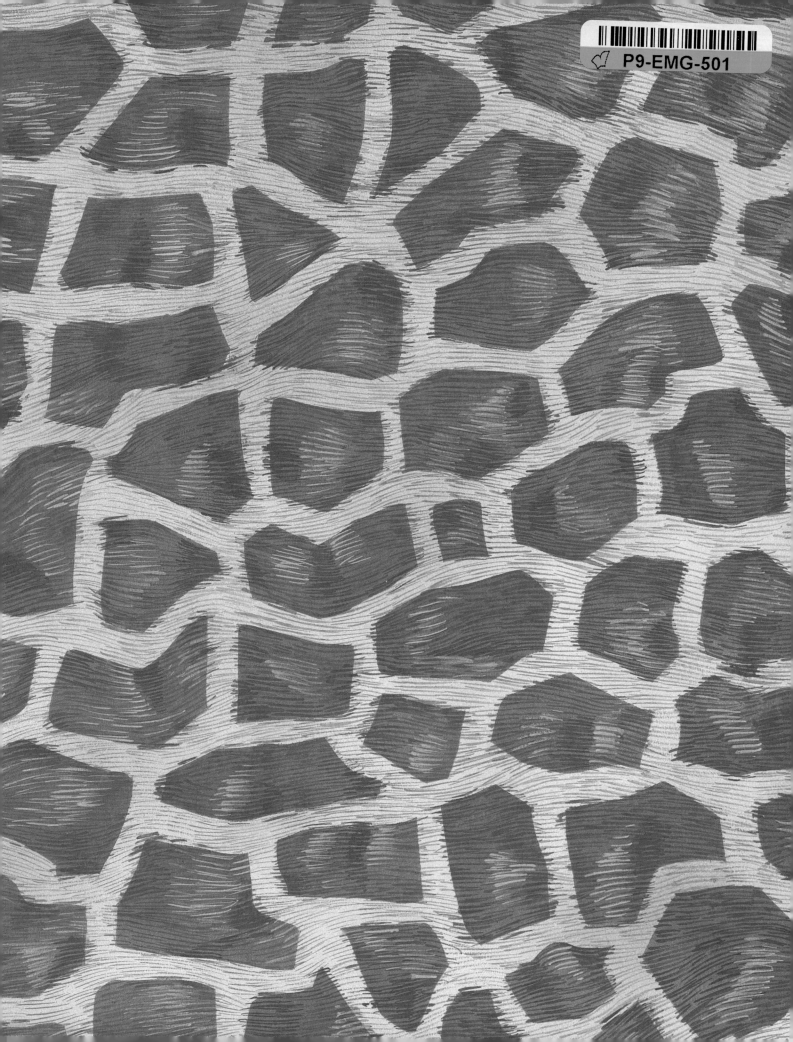

PAPA OB LONG
The Animals' Great Journey

PAPA OB LONG
The Animals' Great Journey

LEROY BLANKENSHIP

Illustrated by
KELLY MAGLADRY

Tommy
NELSON

Thomas Nelson, Inc.
Nashville

Executive Editor: Laura Minchew; Managing Editor: Beverly Phillips; Project Team: Carol Bartley, Marianne Hering.

Library of Congress Cataloging-in-Publication Data

Blankenship, Leroy, 1938-
     Papa Ob Long : the animals' great journey / Leroy Blankenship;
  illustrated by Kelly Magladry.
               p.   cm.
     Summary: Ob Long the giraffe is one of the first animals to hear
of God's plan to gather two of each animal on Noah's ark, and
giraffes ever since have sung of his journey.
     ISBN 0-8499-5824-5
     1. Noah's ark—Juvenile Fiction. [1. Noah's ark—Fiction.
2. Giraffes—Fiction. 3. Animals—Fiction.] I. Magladry, Kelly,
1958- ill. II. Title.
PZ7.B61317Pap   1998
[E]—dc 21
                                                97-44248
                                                CIP
                                                AC

Printed in the United States of America

98 99 00 01 02 03 WCV 9 8 7 6 5 4 3 2 1

The best time to catch a giraffe humming is on a hot summer day. And if you know anything about giraffes, you know they hum only one song. Before a baby giraffe can count its spots, it learns about the animals' great journey and the song of Papa Ob Long.

On the night one special giraffe was born,
the moon glowed gold and warm, declaring
the power of God, the Great Maker.
The grassland animals gathered to welcome
the arrival of the baby giraffe. Like all of
his kind, his legs wobbled when he walked,
and his coat was the color of brown leaves
scattered on harvesttime grass.
No creature knew then
what a special giraffe
he would be.

His parents named him Ob Long, a good and noble name that some said could be traced all the way back to the first giraffes in the Garden of Eden.

As Ob Long grew, and grew, and grew, and grew . . .
he led a simple life. He slept. He wandered. He nibbled
on tender branches and spent the day chewing them.
With his family, he followed the herd to places where the
grass was thick and green and leaves covered the treetops.

One day Ob Long noticed a graceful giraffe named Skippa and fell in love with her. When they married, her name became Skippa Long, and she went with her husband everywhere.

One afternoon as Ob and Skippa

snacked on sweet acacia leaves,

a curious and strange white
butterfly visited the plains.
Such a creature the two
giraffes had never seen
before. It was marvelous . . .

. . . and it landed right on Ob Long's nose. "Ob Long," the butterfly said, "God has need of you. You must bring Skippa and follow me to a faraway land."

Ob Long knew that God cared for all of His creatures, from the tiniest gnat to the mightiest bull elephant. He had no reason to fear the journey, because God would lead the way.

"I wish to please God," Ob Long said politely. "I will leave my home and go wherever He leads me. And there I will become a papa and raise children and grow old—"

"You will not live to grow old,"
the butterfly said with a smile,
"unless you hurry to obey God."

"We will obey now,"
Ob Long answered.

After that, the butterfly flew to a
nearby tree and gave God's message
to the winged creatures. A bee, a swallow,
and a hummingbird at once believed the message
and joined the butterfly. Ob Long watched them
soar away. The wise giraffe trusted the Lord
and followed His call.

The other animals who heard the message
followed too. They knew that God had
created them and would care for them.
From north, east, south, and west came
the wild creatures. Camels, zebras, and birds,
gorillas, elephants, and antelopes crossed
the desert. From all over the earth,
the animals walked, wiggled, or ran,
hopped, flew, or swam to the great gathering.

The wild animals gathered two by two, and at
the end of their journey they saw a man named Noah
with the power of God's Spirit flowing around him.
As they circled around Noah and his very large boat,
Ob Long was given this song:

> The Lord spoke to Noah, to build him a boat.
>
> "Just follow directions, and I'll make it float.
>
> Build it with gopher wood, three stories high."
>
> And when he was finished, the animals came by.

There were lions and leopards, llamas and lynx,

Monkeys and muskrats, mongooses and minks,

Hyenas and hippos, horses and hares,

Badgers and beavers, buffaloes and bears.

Black-and-white zebras followed by skunks,

Then came the elephants, waving their trunks.

Noah stopped for a moment to breathe out a sigh.

But the Lord just kept bringing those animals by.

There were woodchucks and weasels and furry wombats,

Camels, coyotes, cougars, and cats,

Gerbils and gophers, hamsters and hogs,

Polecats and porcupines, donkeys and dogs.

There were pigeons and parrots, a peacock, a peahen,

Redbirds and robins, ravens and wrens.

Noah said, "Lord, I think this will do."

But the Lord kept bringing them two by two.

There were anteaters, anacondas, antelopes, and apes.

Noah said, "Lord, can't You give me a break?

Chinchillas and chipmunks, cheetahs and chimps.

What am I to do with the animals You sent?"

There were reindeer and elk with big, pointed racks,

Brown-speckled and yellow long-necked giraffes,

Orangutans, raccoons—animals galore.

Kangaroos and koalas leaped through the doors.

There were rhinos with horns and big burly backs,

Baboons and caribous and curly-haired yaks,

Gorillas, armadillos, cows, moose, and goats.

So Noah set sail on this three-story boat.

Skippa and Ob Long followed the other animals onto the boat. Even though the rains came and the waves rose so high they nearly swallowed the boat, the animals were safe inside. And they had plenty to eat because God had provided for them.

When the rain stopped and the land dried up,
God painted bright colors across the sky.
Ob Long heard God tell Noah, "The rainbow is a
promise to all living things—to those with wings
and those that walk across the land—that I will
never again destroy the earth with a flood."

Ob Long whispered the good news in a zebra's ear.
The zebra shrieked about the rainbow to
the hippo, and the hippo bellowed it to
one and all. The rest of the day the
chimps swung from tree to tree,
chattering that God loves and
cares for all living creatures.
The ruckus never ended, for
to this day the animals talk
about the goodness of the Lord.

Years later Papa Ob Long
would sing his famous song almost
every day. His grandchildren, Tagga Long and
Hoppa Long, would beg, "Please tell us about
Noah and the boat."

Papa Ob Long would clear his throat as if to
reach the high notes, but he always began with
a lesson. "Look at the rainbow," he would say.
"It is a sign that God loves and cares for every
creature, from the smallest ant to the
tallest giraffe. And He cares for
you too."

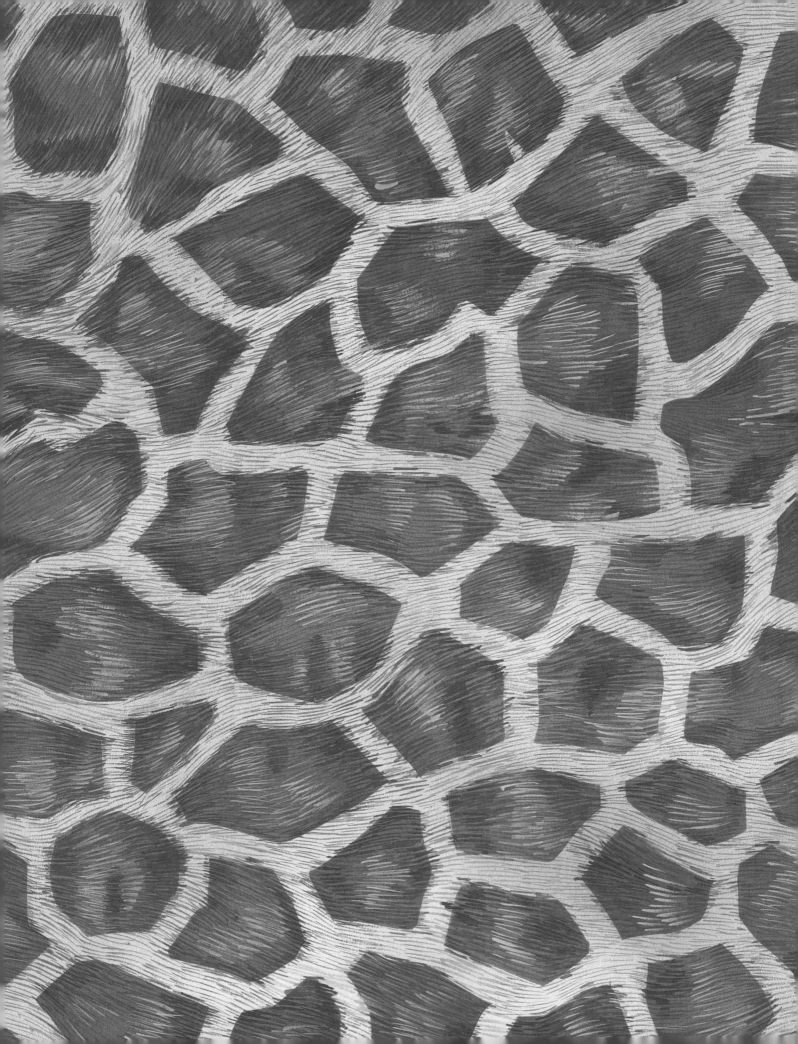